FINNEY . McEVOY . COLBERT . ROCHA

WORLD WAR KAIJU

BOOK ONE: THE COLD WAR YEARS

WORLD WAR KAIJU

BOOK ONE: THE COLD WAR YEARS

Published by 01Publishing.

ISBN 10: 0983923035
ISBN 13: 978-0983923039

www.01Publishing.com

Printed in PRC

Written by Josh Finney

Art by Patrick McEvoy

**Additional scenes, concepts, & dialog by
Michael Colbert**

**Editor
Kat Rocha**

**Copy editors
Lee Finney, Jaycee Baron,
Diane "Dianthrax" Evert,
Gretchen Helms**

**Layout, graphic design, 3D modeling,
and additional page art by Josh Finney**

**Additional character and creature
design by Kat Rocha**

<u>EYES ONLY</u>

SUBJECT:WORLD WAR KAIJI, BOOK ONE.

DOCUMENT PREPARED

BRIEFING OFFICER: JOSH FINNEY (MJ-1)

* * * * * *

DISCLAIMER: The documents contained herein are understood to be a labor of love and a tribute to the kaiju genre in all its forms. The story presented would never have been possible if it were not for the combined visions of Ishiro Honda, Eiji Tsuburaya, Shinichi Sekizawa, and Willis O'Brien. Any likeness to known monsters, celebrities, and political figures (living or dead) is purely intentional and used for the purposes of homage and parody.

MEMO

Dea

you
sp
th
Ma

c
o
with your
Intelligence.

008

CHAPTER ONE

"KING OF THE BEASTS"

August 6th, 1945.

That was the night everything changed.

By then, D-Day had come and gone. We'd dealt with Hitler and Mussolini, and damn near kicked their fascist asses all the way across Europe. But the Japs?

The Japs were holding strong.

J A P A N

TOKYO

Fortunately for us, the lab coats in New Mexico had made the breakthrough we'd all been praying for. They'd managed to hatch Biblical destruction at the push of a button.

The weapon's codename was Fat Man. Of course, after his debut in Tokyo the Japs soon came to know him by a different name...

Ryujin, king of the beasts.

We were gonna sell him to the public as Atomo-Rex, but the brass up at the Pentragon thought, 'fuck it!' The Japs already seemed to have a name for the big guy...

Had to do with some old legend, or so I'm told. Couldn't tell ya if it's true, but there's something to be said for irony, right?

RYU JIN!

The plan was to loose Fat Man on Tokyo, let the lizard smash up some coastal real-estate.

We figured he'd start some fires, stomp some tanks, and generally scare the shit out of the Japs. That said, we really had no idea of how the operation would go down. I mean, we knew he gave off a ton of radiation. That was sure to leave a mark.

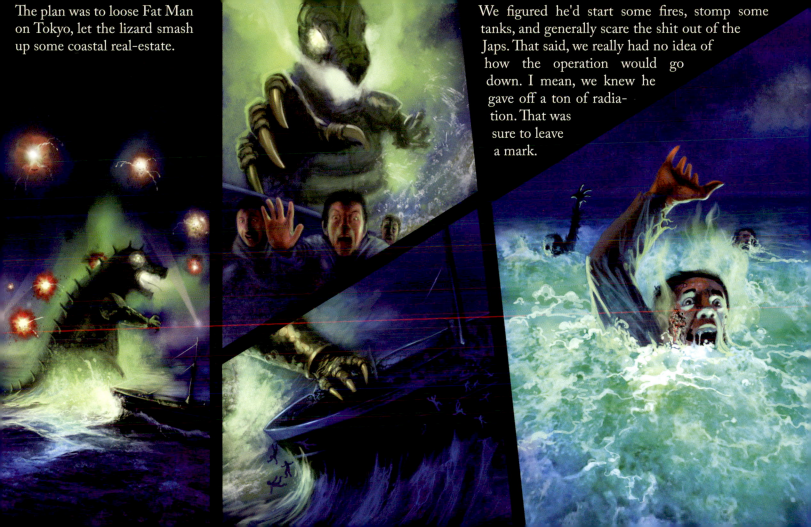

But what we didn't expect was how inventive the big fucker was gonna be.

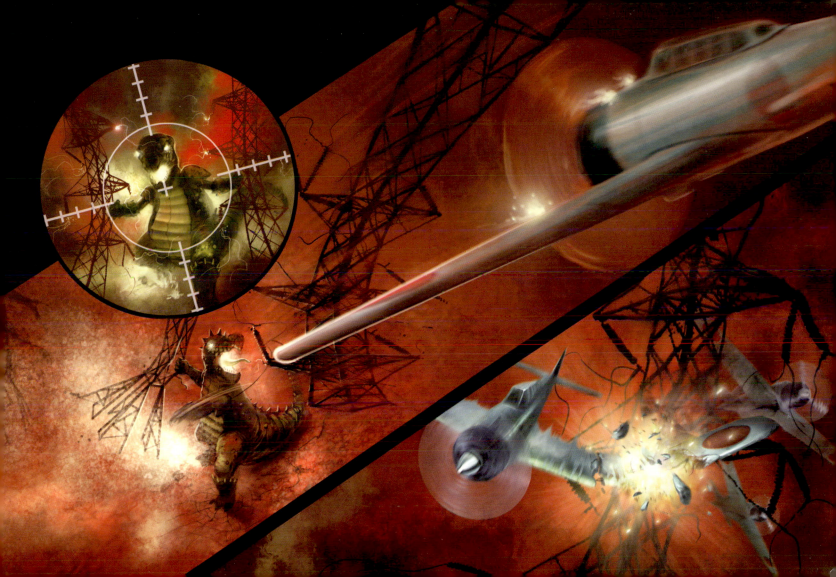

The truth is…

…most Japanese were sick of the war, too.

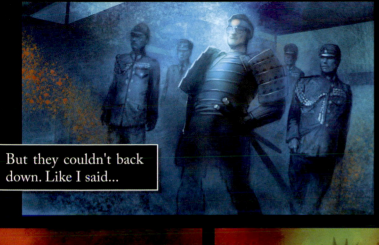

But they couldn't back down. Like I said...

...the Japanese, they're a very proud people. At the time, their culture simply didn't allow for surrender. If America was going to end the war, we were gonna have to hit the Japs so goddamn hard...

FAT MAN TRIUMPHANT. America's historic attack on Tokyo signified the end of the Second World War and the dawn of the Kaiju Age.

The Japs surrendered two days later. It would've been sooner but it took that long to find anybody in authority. They were all either dead, or so scared shitless they'd gone into hiding. I was with Naval Intelligence during the war, which meant I was one of the first Americans in Tokyo after the big guy'd wrecked it.

YOU HAD TO BE THERE TO REALLY UNDERSTAND JUST HOW OLD TESTAMENT THE DEVASTATION WAS.

SCREW ALL THAT 'A SMOLDERING MEMORIAL TO THE UNKNOWN...' TRIPE WHAT'S-HIS-FACE WROTE IN THE PAPERS.

THAT'S ALL WELL AND GOOD, MISTER HAMPTON, BUT ASIDE FROM A PERSONAL TOUCH...

...YOU HAVEN'T SAID A THING I HAVEN'T ALREADY HEARD IN GRADE SCHOOL.

WHEN I AGREED TO THIS INTERVIEW YOU PROMISED TOP SECRET INFORMATION, THE INSIDE SCOOP ON THE NIXON WHITEHOUSE WHEN, AND I'M QUOTING YOU NOW...

"...WHEN THE SHIT REALLY HIT THE FAN."

TRUST ME, KEEGAN, YOU'LL HAVE YOUR SECRETS.

YOU'LL HAVE 'EM IN SPADES.

I'VE GOT A WHOLE LITANY OF CLASSIFIED DATA SO MIND-BENDINGLY FUCKED UP...

...YOUR BALLS ARE GONNA SHRIVEL UP WHEN YOU HEAR IT ALL!

BUT YA CAN'T PUT THE CART BEFORE THE HORSES, ALRIGHT? ROME WASN'T BURNT IN A DAY.

YEAH, BUT TOKYO WAS.

EXACTLY MY POINT, KID! FOR THIS STORY CONTEXT IS EVERYTHING...

HAMPTON: ...and there's a lot of things grade school never taught ya about the kaiju and the arms race...stuff that's been kept from the American people.

KEEGAN: Mister Hampton, you ever heard the old adage, 'If something sounds too good to be true, it probably is?' When a man who's spent twenty years with the CIA calls an acclaimed journalist saying he's willing to offer up top secret information, THAT sounds too good to be true. Now your credentials *do* check out. You *are* who you *say* you are. But so far, Mister Hampton, all you've done is waste my time with old war stories. For all I know, you're just some spook here to discredit my work by feeding me false information.

HAMPTON: Jesus! I wish you twerps in the press were half as skeptical about the stuff *you* print as fact! As for what I got to say, just show me a little patience. This story requires some set-up, alright? I'm sure an *acclaimed* journalist such as yourself can handle *that* much. But if it helps any, I will give you the moral of the story right now.

KEEGAN: And that is?

HAMPTON: After we loosed Fat Man on Tokyo we should've come clean with the American people, told 'em everything we knew about this awesome force we'd unleashed. Maybe then it would've been different. Maybe there wouldn't have been a Third World War.

KEEGAN: That's what my generation has been saying for years, old man! You squares just haven't been listening.

C'MON, MAN!

YOU GOVERNMENT CREEPS WOKE UP MONSTERS! HOW COULD YOU EXPECT THERE *NOT* TO BE...

...CONSEQUENCES?!

SIBERIA, 1949. An omnious mushroom cloud rises above the Semipalatinsk Test Site as Russia successfully hatches its first KAI-235 crystal.

HAMPTON: Lotta as weren't as thick skulled as you think, Keegan. Anyone paying attention knew there'd be consequences. But what we were doing back then, you gotta think of it like war bonds; ya get what you need to survive *now* and hope you're alive to pay for it in the future. We did the best we could. Sure, the country's a wreck, but we still have food on our plates and roofs over our heads.

KEEGAN: So is this the part where you say, "Pleased to meet you, hope you guess my name?"

HAMPTON: <*laughs*> And *that's* why it has to be you, Keegan. I've read your stuff in *Rolling Rock Magazine*, or whatever the hell it's called. You're as anti-establishment as they come, but you're also honest. Listened to enough of your wiretaps to know as much. I figure if anyone can wake up the Love Generation to what's going on, it's you.

KEEGAN: Okay, okay... So what's this truth that's gonna blow my mind?

HAMPTON: Where to start? There's so much to tell. After the war...the second one, that is...things got real stupid, real fast. With Hitler and Tojo gone the clowns up in Washington were just so damn sure we were sitting pretty. 'We got the beast! Whose gonna challenge us now?!' was the myth of the day. Presumptuous assholes. It was too late, the genie was out of the bottle! It was only a matter of time before the Reds made some kaiju of their own.

VOL. CXLX   No. 654

AUGUST 30th, 1949

Russia Has The Beast!

World shocked by Kremlin's announcement! America's security no longer certain!

Fiv

..COW -- Democratic nations across ...obe now must live in the shadow of a ...rror as the peace and security of the ...orld is no longer certain. Yesterday ...iet Union successfully hatched a ...nctioning, war-ready kaiju monster. ...drupedal spiked-back creature, ...he "Red Armadillo," is said to be ...on beast measuring more that ...a length. "If what the Soviets are ...s to be believed this Armadillo ...theirs is roughly the same size ...as our biggest kaiju, Gorzira," ...n spokesman, Major Anthony ...ding expert in the field of ...Major Nelson said there was ...bout the true capabilities of ...unist threat. "It is critical

once a city of six million people. What happened here has been caused by a fo which up until a few days ago was entire beyond the scope of man's imagination. smoldering memorial to the unknown, a unknown which at this very moment stil prevails and which could at anytime lash out with its terrible destruction anywhere else in the world. There

**NEWSREEL
TRANSCRIPT:**
Dateline August,
1949! *Siberia!*
The Reds unlock
the secrets of
the beast! They call
him the Red Armadillo! And
according to Ivan he's bigger
and loads meaner than Uncle
Sam's space-age dino, Fat Man!

THE RED ARMADILLO! HA!

WHAT A FUCKING JOKE!

HAMPTON: Our first try we produced Fat Man, the meanest motherfucker to ever walk the Earth. What'd the Russians make? A clumsy tail dragger that squealed like a pig! You know the Armadillo's skin wasn't even red? The Ruskies painted him up! Even riveted all those stupid horns on his back to make him look more formidable. Dumb bastards. *<laughs>*

Of course, the Armadillo wasn't what had us worried. We'd had kaiju failures of our own... Christ, just look at that freak, Little Boy. I don't think the Pentagon ever managed to convince anyone he was anything other than a walking, belching, thirty foot tall radioactive embarrassment. Frankly, the less said about "The Son of Fat Man," the better.

But like I said, when the Reds got the beast, it wasn't Red Armadillo that had everyone worried. Nah, the real fear came down to a matter of real-estate. You wanted secrets, right? Here's one; Siberia is packed full of KAI-235 crystals. The region's just crammed with the damn things, which is exactly why it didn't take long for the Reds to outpace us in the arms race. For every kaiju we hatched, the commies could produce at least two or three. Far as quantity, they had our asses beat. Quality, on the other hand, let's just say they're better at making vodka.

Which brings me to an important point; you ever stop and wonder how it is a crystal that's been resting under the Earth, or at the bottom of the ocean, for the last fifty million years can be bombarded with protons and somehow become a Fat Man or an Armadillo? Seriously, just stop and think about that for a moment. Do you realize how utterly impossible that all sounds? Our scientists are capable of some amazing feats, but c'mon! We didn't figure out the photocopier until '59!

TRINITY hatching No.2, CODENAME: Little Boy

YEAH, WELL I THOUGHT IT WAS THE NAZIS WHO'D MADE MOST OF THE BREAKTHROUGHS AND...

...THE PENTAGON JUST GAVE THEM JOBS.

HAMPTON: Fuck, kid! Would you've rather they'd spilled their secrets to the Russians? Open your damn eyes! It's not a nice world! It's not like someday we'll all share a Coke on top of a mountain and sing some dumb ass song in perfect harmony. There are plenty of monsters in the world who aren't of the atomic variety. They look like us, act like us, and they hate everything this nation stands for.

KEEGAN: The Russians, you mean.

HAMPTON: Nah. I *like* the goddamn Russians, truth be told. Us and them got a lot in common. They're like the mouthy kid in school who's always gotta one up ya, so you're always gettin' in fights. Nah... It ain't the Reds who worry me anymore. Plus their women fuck like beasts! Ya gotta love 'em for that. But I'm getting off track...what was I talking about again?

KEEGAN: Monsters hatching from kai crystals.

HAMPTON: Oh. Right. Like I was saying... True, it was the Krauts who'd figured out the glow inside a kai crystal contained life...or at least something that could become life. And slamming it with protons the right way would hatch it like an egg. But that still doesn't answer the obvious question, which is, how's that even possible? Einstein himself said it defies just about everything we know about matter and energy. Heck, after all these years we still don't know why the hatching process works. We just know it does.

And for that matter, how the hell did the Krauts get the idea in the first place? Seriously! You look at history, discovery tends to have a logical progression. Newton and his apple. Darwin's voyage. Sekizawa and his oxygen studies. You can see how these men got from point A to point B in their research. But Project Fenris? It's like one day the Krauts woke up and just knew monsters could be spawned from a kai crystal.

KEEGAN: What is it are you implying?

HAMPTON: Nothing. It's a mystery.

KEEGAN: And the Nazi scientists now working at the Pentagon? They didn't shed any light on the matter? I know damn well your CIA buddies interrogated every one of those scientists. I interviewed Von Braun a few years back. The man didn't have a nice thing to say about the lot of you.

PROJECT FENRIS. During the Second World War, Hitler's scientists raced to perfect a functioning kaiju weapon.

Although the program made great strides it never managed to hatch anything beyond a single malformed kaiju, which died shortly after its creation. Fenris was fortunately cut short in 1943 when the British RAF staged a daring raid on the project's labs on the Ruhr.

...HAMPTON: Yeah, well, poor Werner Von Braun, I think he felt picked on. All day he'd be working with hotshot astronauts who loved yanking his chain, always playing pranks on him, always callin' him stuff like Das Uber Snoz and Herr Rocketman. Then he'd come home to an apartment he knew was bugged and watched. Poor fucker couldn't even go to a movie without a couple spooks camped in the row behind him. Can you blame the man for hating The Company? Heh, you know when ol' Von Braun had a particularly bad day he'd pick-up the phone, knowing it was tapped, and just ramble into the receiver! The wiretap boys had a ball with him. But yeah, we did grill every egghead Kraut who came over to our side. Lot of them did have pretty bizarre tales to tell. Most left us with more questions than

answers, though. And for any of their oddball stories to make a shred of sense, we're first gonna have to discuss Mohdrah.

KEEGAN: *Mohdrah?* Why Mohdrah?

HAMPTON: Remember Mohdrah's big splash onto the world stage? That dumb ass stunt she pulled with the UN?

KEEGAN: Remember? Mohdrah's sacrifice is a rallying call for my generation, old man. It virtually inspired the peace movement. What Mohdrah did was the ultimate sit-in. She single-handedly ended the war in Korea through non-violent means. She gave her life for peace...

A moment in the life of Wernher Von Braun, godfather of modern rocketry.

HAMPTON: Yeah, and none of you were older than five when it happened! If Mohdrah had struck while *Howdy Doody* was on, none of you would've even remembered it! Your generation's rallying call is revisionist history. Trust me on this...that fucking bug was neither a pacifist nor a protector. It's a giant pain in the ass. Mohdrah's so-called "sit-in" had nothing to do with the Korean War. Her little PR duo all but said as much...

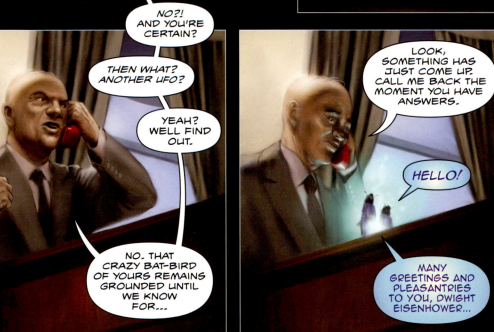

IS IT RUSSIAN?

NO?! AND YOU'RE CERTAIN?

THEN WHAT? ANOTHER UFO?

YEAH? WELL FIND OUT.

NO. THAT CRAZY BAT-BIRD OF YOURS REMAINS GROUNDED UNTIL WE KNOW FOR...

LOOK, SOMETHING HAS JUST COME UP. CALL ME BACK THE MOMENT YOU HAVE ANSWERS.

HELLO!

MANY GREETINGS AND PLEASANTRIES TO YOU, DWIGHT EISENHOWER...

...WISE ELDER AND ELECTED LEADER OF THE UNITED AMERICAN STATES!

YOU MUST LISTEN TO WHAT WE HAVE TO SAY!

NOW LET ME ASK YOU THIS, EITHER OF YOU GIRLS HAPPEN TO KNOW ABOUT THE *THING* THAT'S BEEN FLYING UP AND DOWN THE EAST COAST ALL DAY? A *THING* THAT'S FASTER THAN OUR BEST JETS, YET BIGGER THAN THIS BUILDING?

WHY YES! THE THING YOU SPEAK OF IS CALLED MOHDRAH.

SHE IS A GUARDIAN AND PROTECTOR OF THE EARTH.

SHE HAS COME ALL THE WAY FROM OUR HOME ON DINKI ISLAND TO SHOW MANKIND YOU MUST STOP YOUR EVIL WAYS!

NOW THAT SHE KNOWS THAT NEITHER THE UNION OF SOVIETS OR THE AMERICAN STATES WILL DO AWAY WITH THEIR KAIJU MONSTERS...

...MOHDRAH IS FLYING TO YOUR UNITED NATIONS IN THE GREAT CITY OF NEW YORK TO PLEAD FOR PEACE!

AND HOW WILL THIS GIANT BUG...

...MAKE HER PLEA, EXACTLY?

MOHDRAH WILL WEAVE A BEAUTIFUL WEB OF PEACE AROUND YOUR UNITED NATIONS AND COCOON HERSELF TO THERE!

NO ONE WILL BE...

...ABLE TO LEAVE UNLESS ALL THE WORLD PROMISES TO CEASE DOING EVIL AND NEVER AGAIN MAKE KAIJU!

AND MOHDRAH IS ABOUT TO DO THIS RIGHT NOW?!

OH YES!

WE WISH FOR HUMANITY TO HAVE GREAT PEACE AND HAPPINESS!

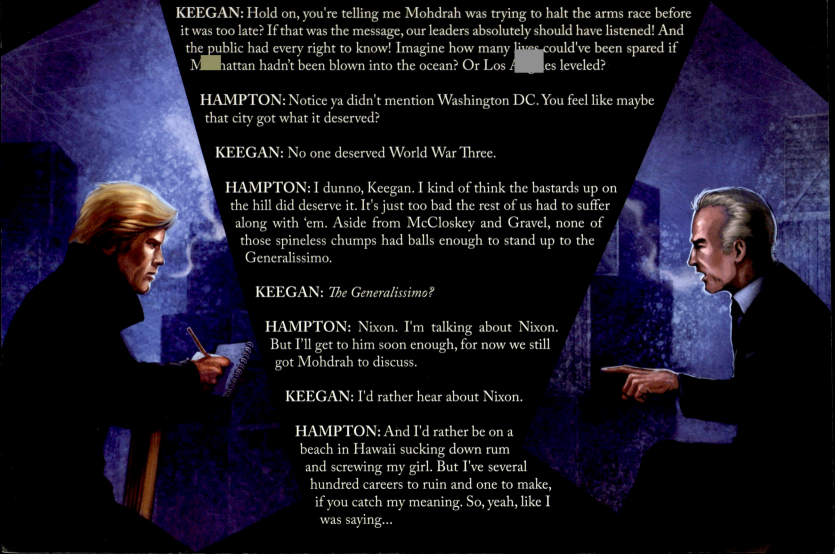

KEEGAN: Hold on, you're telling me Mohdrah was trying to halt the arms race before it was too late? If that was the message, our leaders absolutely should have listened! And the public had every right to know! Imagine how many lives could've been spared if M███hattan hadn't been blown into the ocean? Or Los A███es leveled?

HAMPTON: Notice ya didn't mention Washington DC. You feel like maybe that city got what it deserved?

KEEGAN: No one deserved World War Three.

HAMPTON: I dunno, Keegan. I kind of think the bastards up on the hill did deserve it. It's just too bad the rest of us had to suffer along with 'em. Aside from McCloskey and Gravel, none of those spineless chumps had balls enough to stand up to the Generalissimo.

KEEGAN: *The Generalissimo?*

HAMPTON: Nixon. I'm talking about Nixon. But I'll get to him soon enough, for now we still got Mohdrah to discuss.

KEEGAN: I'd rather hear about Nixon.

HAMPTON: And I'd rather be on a beach in Hawaii sucking down rum and screwing my girl. But I've several hundred careers to ruin and one to make, if you catch my meaning. So, yeah, like I was saying...

...Mohdrah took the UN hostage to back up her vague and poorly communicated demand that the nations of the world curb their kaiju warfare programs. Naturally, this pissed Ike off to no end.

DID...

DID THEY JUST VANISH?

SHIT! GET THE AIR FORCE ON THE HORN!

NOW!

So Ike gave the green light to drop Razor Beak into the fray.

Razor Beak...
   Jesus, now there was one mean son of a bitch. Ever stare into eyes of a crocodile? Notice how there ain't a trace of empathy in 'em. You look at a croc, you know it's only got three thoughts cycling through its brain—kill, eat, shit. Same fucking thing with Razor Beak. That beast had nothing between the ears but cold, primal carnage.

If Ike wanted to let Mohdrah know what he thought of her diplomacy methods, I think Razor Beak more than got the point across.

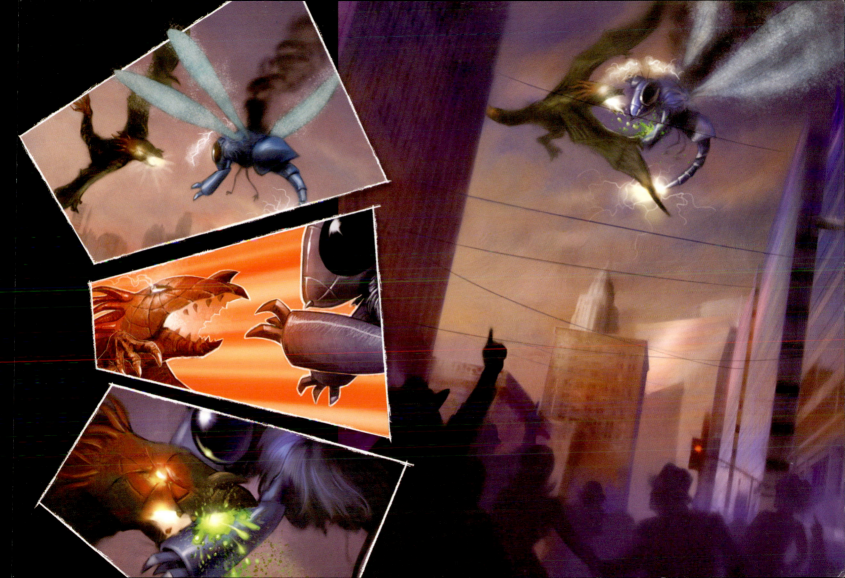

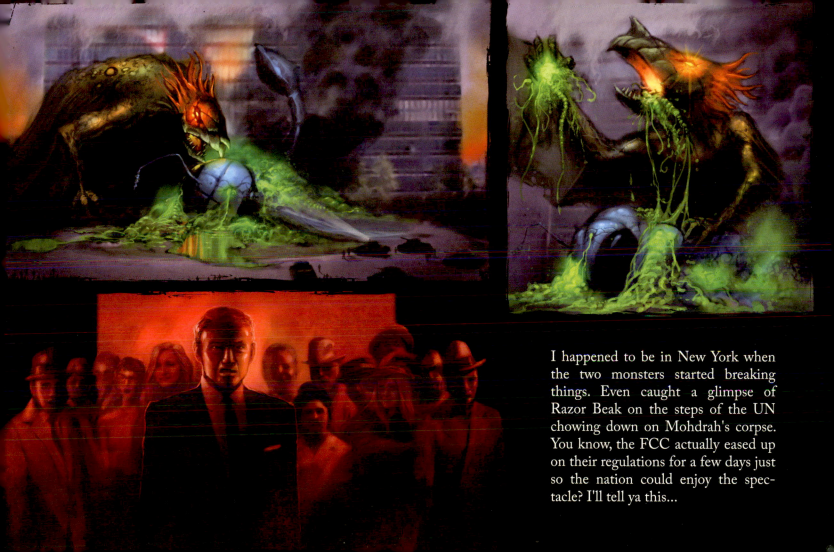

I happened to be in New York when the two monsters started breaking things. Even caught a glimpse of Razor Beak on the steps of the UN chowing down on Mohdrah's corpse. You know, the FCC actually eased up on their regulations for a few days just so the nation could enjoy the spectacle? I'll tell ya this...

HAMPTON: ...one thing they never mention about kaiju is how bad they smell, especially when one's been lasered in half and its green guts are smoldering on hot July pavement. Maybe it's just psychosomatic, but I swear I still can't pass the UN plaza without getting a faint wiff of charred Mohdrah.

KEEGAN: Smell anything like the toy?

HAMPTON: Toy? I'm afraid you've lost me.

KEEGAN: That Christmas it was what every boy begged his parents for, the *NYC Monster Battle* playset. It came with green-scented Mohdrah guts that glowed in the dark. They always ended up getting rubbed into the carpet which resulted in some very upset mothers.

HAMPTON: No shit? They made toys outta that? Jesus, now that is some serious avarice right there. No wonder kids're so screwed up nowadays. Whatever happened to just getting junior a cowboy hat and a pair of six-shooters, huh? But anyway, yeah, that was Mohdrah's debut on the world stage, however confused and poorly executed it was. You know, the ironic part is after the voting public found out there were rogue monsters out there willing to take terrorist action on US soil, well, anyone who was lukewarm

about the arms build-up quickly changed their tune.

KEEGAN: I'm sure the Whitehouse's smear campaign did a lot to drive public sentiment.

HAMPTON: I won't bullshit you. After the fact, there was a concerted effort to make Mohdrah the scapegoat, which wasn't hard considering she'd taken down the 9th Street Bridge on her way in. Wiping out a busy thoroughfare full of commuters will get you some bad fucking press.

KEEGAN: And the millions of dollars of collateral damage caused by Razorbeak interceding?

HAMPTON: Hey, ya get creatures that immense tussling in a major city, you're gonna see some real estate values fall. It's inevitable.

KEEGAN: Okay. So what is it you're not telling me, Hampton?

HAMPTON: I dunno. What is it you're not asking?

KEEGAN: *<pauses>* During the attack. You guys learned something, didn't you? Something you purposely kept out of the public eye.

YOU'RE CLOSE. DAMN CLOSE...

HAMPTON: When the Pixies made their appeal to Ike...before things got stupid, that is...they rattled off a tale that was both hard to believe, yet made perfect sense. And regardless of what anyone thinks, we took it seriously enough to keep the information locked up tight for more than two decades. What I'm about to tell you is classified above top secret. Just by admitting this information exists I'm committing an act of treason. What happened is...

TO UNDERSTAND THE PRESENT YOU...

...MUST FIRST KNOW THE PAST.

LONG AGO, BEFORE HUMANS WALKED THE EARTH, A GREAT CIVILIZATION LIVED AMONGST THE STARS.

KNOWN TO ALL AS THE ZIOX...

...THEY WERE A BRILLIANT PEOPLE WHOSE SCIENCE AND INVENTIONS FAR SURPASSED...

...THOSE OF EARTH.

SADLY, THOUGH...

...IS PLANET EARTH.

YEAH.

I'VE READ ENOUGH ISSUES OF STRANGE TALES IN MY YOUTH TO KNOW WHERE YOU'RE GOING WITH THIS. AND THIS IS WHEN I SAY...

FUCK YOU VERY MUCH FOR WASTING MY FRIDAY EVENING.

I'LL BE GOING NOW.

SIT YOUR ASS BACK DOWN!

YOU'RE WILLING TO ACCEPT A WORLD POPULATED BY TELEPORTING PIXIES AND GIANT PEACENIK BUGS, YET SPACEMEN ARE WHERE YOU...

DRAW THE FUCKING LINE?!

YEAH.

ME AND ABOUT 90% OF AMERICANS DO! AND UNLIKE YOUR SPACEMEN, HAMPTON, THE PIXIES ARE REALLY REAL. EVERYBODY'S SEEN 'EM! THEY'VE BEEN ON CARSON, WHAT? TWO? THREE TIMES?! BUT ANCIENT ASTRONAUTS?! C'MON! IT'S A KOOK THEORY, JUST LIKE THE ATOM BOMB, TIME TRAVEL, AND ALL THAT.

YA KNOW, I DON'T GET IT. MAYBE IT'S ME. MAYBE...

...IT'S THE GENERATION GAP. BUT I DON'T GET YOU KIDS AT ALL. TIM LEARY GETS WHACKED OUT OF HIS GOURD ON LSD AND HAS VISIONS OF MOHDRAH DRY HUMPING STONEHENGE AND YOU KIDS ALL ACCEPT IT AS PROOF THE BUG IS AN EARTH SPIRIT! I GIVE YOU A MORE PLAUSIBLE EXPLANATION, AND I'M A FUCKING ASSHOLE!

CHAPTER TWO

"SCIENCE TASKFORCE, GO!"

WILD STUFF, EH MISTER PRESIDENT?

I'LL TELL YOU THIS, GENTLEMEN...

...FOR BETTER OR FOR ILL...

...WHATEVER HAPPENS HERE TONIGHT, IT WILL BE CUSSED AND DISCUSSED FOR MANY YEARS TO COME.

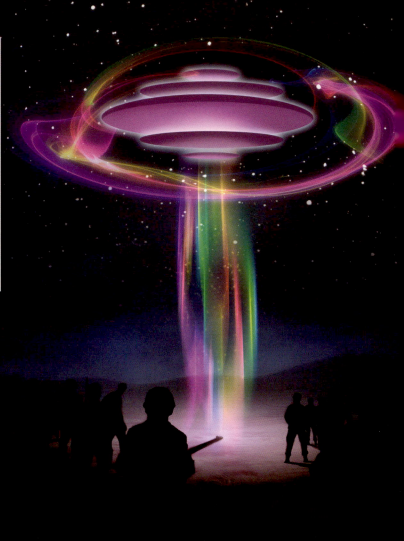

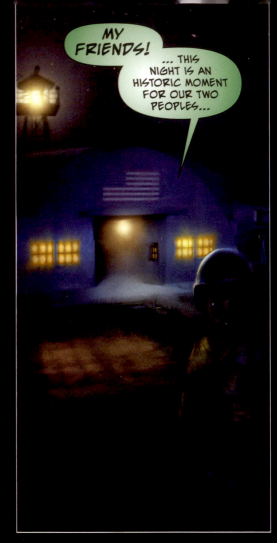

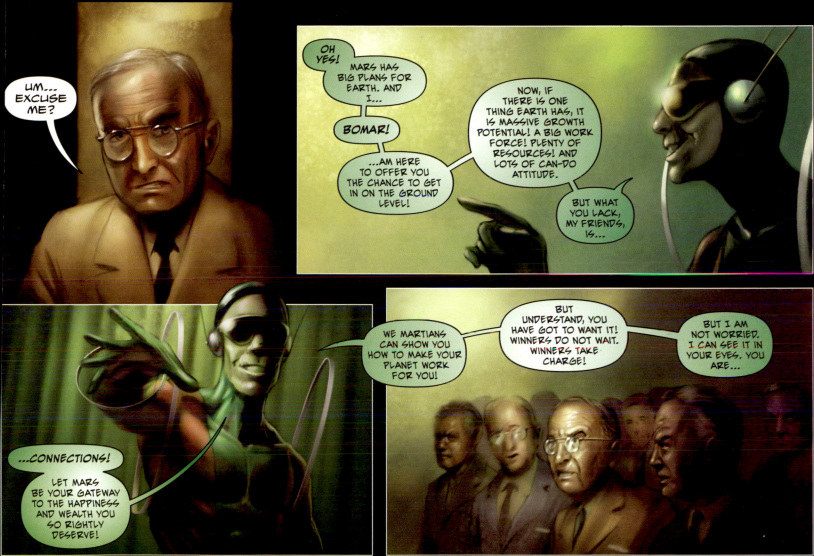

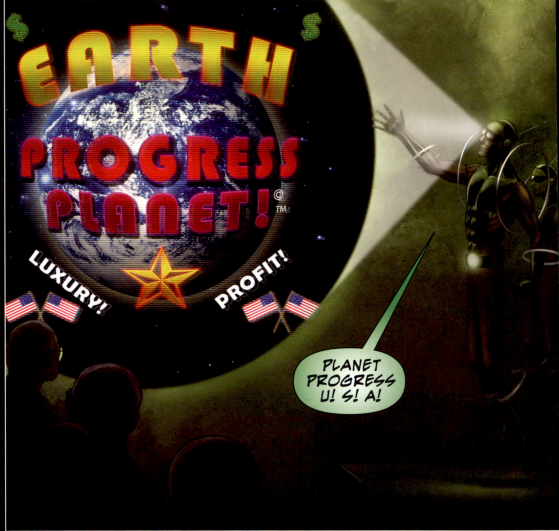

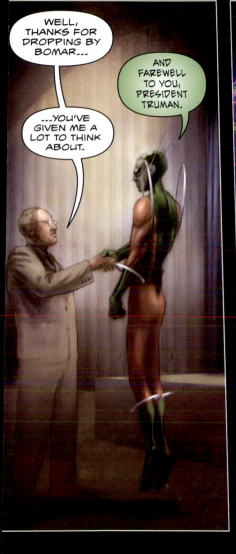

WELL, THANKS FOR DROPPING BY BOMAR...

...YOU'VE GIVEN ME A LOT TO THINK ABOUT.

AND FAREWELL TO YOU, PRESIDENT TRUMAN.

WHAT DO YOU MAKE OF IT, HARRY?

PLAIN HOKUM, JAMES.

OLDEST POLITICAL TRICK IN THE BOOK...

IF YOU CAN'T CONVINCE SOMEONE, CONFUSE 'EM!

THESE MARTIANS ARE NOTHING BUT COMMON HUCKSTERS.

SO WHAT NOW?

WE BLOW THOSE NO GOOD SHITBIRDS OUTTA THE SKY!

Roswell Daily Record

RECORD PHONES
Business Office 2288
News Deprtment
2287

6c PER CO

ROSWELL, NEW MEXICO.   TUESDAY, JULY 8, 1947

ESTABLISHED 1985

RAAF Captures Flying Sauce On Ranch in Roswell Region

Claims Army Is Stacking Court Martial

Indiana Senator Lays Protest Before Patterson

House Passes | Security Council Paves Way to Talks

No Details of Flying Disk

Ex-King Carol Weds Mme. Lupescu

THERE ARE BILLIONS UPON BILLIONS OF STARS IN OUR UNIVERSE. SOME SURELY *MUST* HAVE PLANETS SUITABLE FOR LIFE, AND SHOULD OPTIMISTIC ESTIMATES PREVAIL, SOME OF THEM MUST ALSO SHELTER NEARBY TECHNICAL CIVILIZATIONS...

...AS MANY AS POSSIBLY ONE IN EVERY MILLION STARS IN THE MILKY WAY.

EVEN SO, THE NEAREST ONE WOULD STILL BE A FEW HUNDRED LIGHT YEARS DISTANT...

...MORE LIKELY, THOUGH, A THOUSAND LIGHT YEARS. BUT SPACE IS VAST AND THE STARS ARE FAR.

SO, THE LIKELIHOOD OF A NEARBY CIVILIZATION VISITING US IS...

...VERY, HIGHLY UNLIKELY.

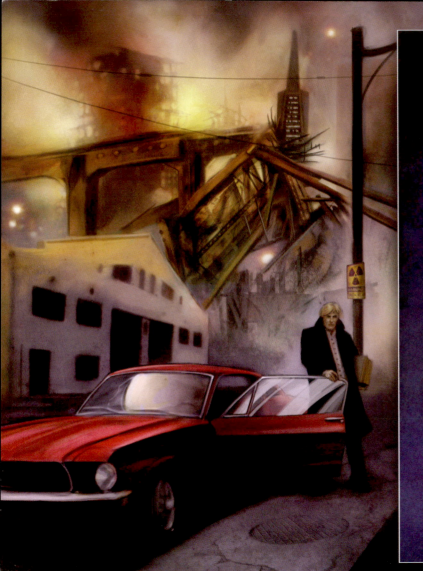

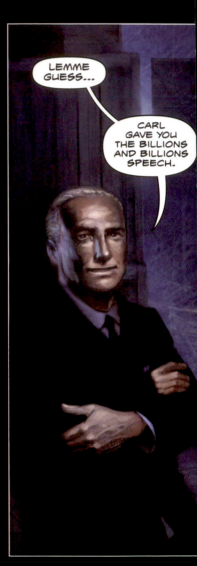

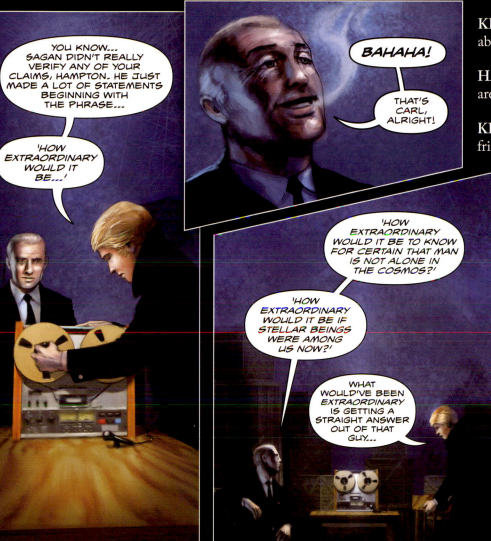

KEEGAN: ...but he sure did like to talk, just not about anything I wanted to know.

HAMPTON: Son, he told you plenty! You're here, aren't ya?

KEEGAN: Yeah, well, I did a little digging on your friend, Mr. Sagan. You know, for a hippy academic he sure has a lot of ties to the military... specifically the Air Force. I also find it interesting that in 1952, Secretary of State Acheson met with Doctor Sagan personally to discuss, and I'm quoting, "How the United States should respond if flying saucers turned out to be extra-terrestrial." And this happened right after the Mohdrah Incident.

HAMPTON: <*chuckles*> You're making it easy for me, kid. Figured I was gonna have to explain all that myself then watch you not believe me again.

KEEGAN: Records also show that around the same time something of a rift began to form between the Administration and the CIA. And know what else I found? *You were there, Hampton.* You were part of this. What happened?

HAMPTON: Heh...yeah, well, I wouldn't call it so much of a rift, but rather a line in the sand

DAMMIT, ALLEN! WHY WASN'T I TOLD?!

TO BE SPECIFIC, SIR...

...WE ONLY KNEW ABOUT THE MARTIANS. AT THE CIA, WE KNEW NOTHING ABOUT THESE *ZIOX* BEINGS YOUR PIXIES SPOKE OF.

I'LL TELL YOU THIS, ALLEN...

I'M READY TO KICK YOU SO FAR DOWN THE FOOD CHAIN YOU'LL HAVE PLANKTON BITES ON YOUR BACKSIDE!

DO YOU REALIZE, UP 'TIL NOW ALL THESE FLYING DISCS WE'VE BEEN SPOTTING...I WAS CERTAIN THEY WERE *RUSSIAN!!*

A MISTAKE LIKE THAT COULD SPARK A WAR, FOR CHRIST'S SAKE!

NO MORE EXCUSES, ALLEN! THIS TIME TOMORROW I EXPECT ALL THE CIA'S FILES ON THIS DESK!

I DON'T CARE HOW WEIRD THEY GET...

SPACEMEN!

SAUCERS!

DEAD COWS!

I WANT THE WHOLE SHEBANG!

MISTER PRESIDENT...

I'M SORRY, BUT I MUST REFUSE. TO EVEN ADMIT SUCH FILES EXIST...

...WOULD DO UNTOLD DAMAGE TO THE NATION'S SECURITY.

HAMPTON: Back at the agency, a favorite line ours was, 'I can neither confirm nor deny.' V tacked that bullshit on to everything. 'I can neith confirm nor deny Ché is a double agent.' 'I c neither confirm nor deny mercenaries were hired blow up the Big Bopper's plane.' So while I c neither confirm nor deny it, I heard Ike punch Allen's lights out. Kicked his ass right there in t. Oval Office.

KEEGAN: Why not just fire the guy?

HAMPTON: It's complicated...politics most. Allen had a lot of powerful friends, not to mentic a brother who *was* the Secretary of State. Was a b. situation all the way around.

KEEGAN: Did Eisenhower get the files?

HAMPTON: What files? You can't requisitic what doesn't officially exist, even if you *are* th President of the United States. I'll tell you th much, Manhattan may've taken a beating durir the attack, but the thing Mohdrah absolute. destroyed was trust inside the White House.

KEEGAN: Nothing like a crisis to show who you real friends are, eh?

HAMPTON: Or generate bad blood. Then again

hat is one of The Company's specialties...suspicion and fear are always good for business. Anyways, when all was said and done, like found himself between a rock and a hard place. Rogue monsters, terrorist pixies, UFOs buzzing the Whitehouse...

KEEGAN: ....and a Central Intelligence Agency he couldn't control. An agency *you* were an active employee of. I'll be upfront with you, Hampton. I'm sensing a lot of omission here. Usually when someone spills their guts, they aren't conspicuously absent from their own story. But you? *You're practically a ghost, man.* Why is that? There something you want to hide?

HAMPTON: Alright... Alright... Ya really wanna know? I was piloting a desk in Langley, spending my days converting coffee into urine. It was garbage work, but ironically...

KEEGAN: Hold up. You said you were a field agent.

HAMPTON: I *was,* until that goddamn bug made her grand entry and took a monster-sized shit all over my career. Recall, I was in Manhattan when Mohdrah and Razor Beak went *mano a mano.*

KEEGAN: Yeah, you and about hundred thousand other people.

HAMPTON: But none of them were Intelligence. You're a newsman, you know how it is. Eyewitness accounts aren't worth fuck-all. The average guy's memory is about as trustworthy as Dean Martin's cock. But me? I've been trained to remember. Events, details, facts—*I'm a goddamn human camera!*

KEEGAN: I still don't see how...

HAMPTON: Fuck, kid. Two monsters fighting? It'd never happened before! And for a long while, I was the only guy in government who'd actually seen two kaijus beat on each other. So yeah, I went from being a *field agent* to an *intelligence asset* almost overnight...deemed "too valuable" to be let out of country. I wasn't happy about being an emasculated office shmuck, but it did make me privy to a lot of Washington drama. Truth is, though, it's Ike I should thank. The man spared my ass from a career of mediocrity when he smacked that son of a bitch Dulles. One black eye, that's what got me out of headquarters.

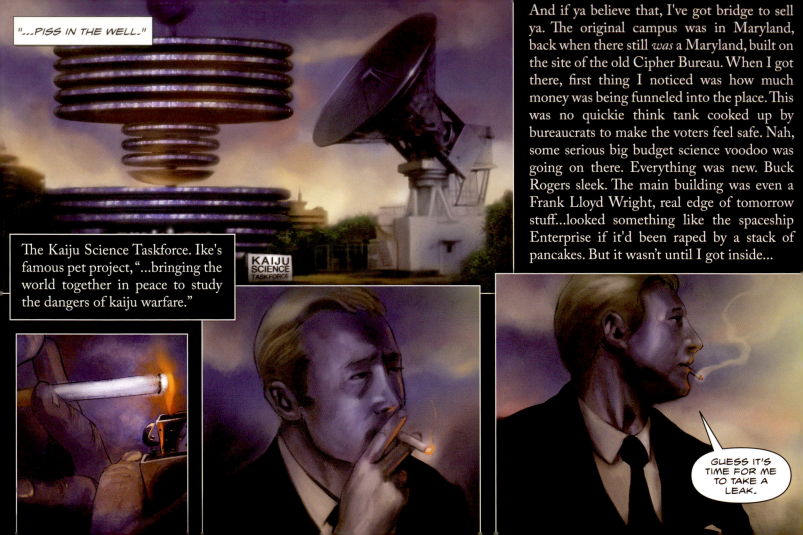

"...PISS IN THE WELL."

The Kaiju Science Taskforce. Ike's famous pet project, "...bringing the world together in peace to study the dangers of kaiju warfare."

KAIJU
SCIENCE
TASKFORCE

And if ya believe that, I've got bridge to sell ya. The original campus was in Maryland, back when there still *was* a Maryland, built on the site of the old Cipher Bureau. When I got there, first thing I noticed was how much money was being funneled into the place. This was no quickie think tank cooked up by bureaucrats to make the voters feel safe. Nah, some serious big budget science voodoo was going on there. Everything was new. Buck Rogers sleek. The main building was even a Frank Lloyd Wright, real edge of tomorrow stuff...looked something like the spaceship Enterprise if it'd been raped by a stack of pancakes. But it wasn't until I got inside...

GUESS IT'S TIME FOR ME TO TAKE A LEAK.

MORNING, GENTLEMEN!

I'M HERE TO SEE THE LEAD EGGHEAD OF THIS CRAZY OUTFIT...

...DOC TSUBURAYA!

YOU HIM?

I'M...

WAIT, LET ME GUESS...

YOU MUST BE AGENT HAMPTON...

...THE MAN ASSIGNED TO US BY YOUR CIA.

I'VE BEEN TOLD YOU'RE THE AGENCY'S NUMBER ONE "KAIJU GUY."

DID ALLEN SAY THAT?

ABOUT ME?

AW, HE'S JUST BEING NICE.

YEAH, I'VE SEEN AN ATOMIC DINO, OR TWO, IN MY TIME.

EXCELLENT!

ASIDE FROM DOCTOR MUHAMMAD AND MYSELF, NONE OF THE STAFF HERE HAS REAL LIFE MONSTER EXPERIENCE.

FIELD WORK? BUDDY, I GOT THAT IN SPADES.

NEW YORK.

TOKYO.

I SAW 'EM BOTH, UP CLOSE AND PERSONAL!

HEY...

...JUST BETWEEN YOU AND ME, THE STAFF HERE ARE MOSTLY WORKER BEES.

I NEED A MAN WHO CAN HANDLE HIMSELF IN A TIGHT SPOT. TELL ME...

CAN YOU SWIM?

It was a real coup getting me onboard. The President was adamant this not be a spying operation. He eventually relented, though when Prescott Bush came calling. It doesn't matter who ya are, in politics you just don't say 'no' to your number one campaign contributor. My being there was justified under the auspices of being the CIA's leading kaiju expert. <laughs> Christ, I was about as much a real expert as J. Edgar was a real woman.

Doc was a product of Hiroshima University, which was and still is the place to be if ya want to know kaiju. The man was also responsible for some of the finest anti-kaiju hardware ever made, such as the Type-88 Telsa tank and the jumbo-sized bear trap.

I remember folks used to ask what it was like working along side a genuine Nobel Prize winning genius like Tsubaraya. You know what I'd say to them? I'd tell 'em it was...

...a shit tornado straight to Oz.

Kaiju Science Taskforce
CASE FILE No. 55
"Case of the Aztec Robo[t]"

Kaiju Science Taskforce
CASE FILE No. 12
"Case of the MegaGator"

Kaiju Science Taskforce
CASE FILE No. 23
"Case of the Winged Death"

Kaiju Science Taskforce
CASE FILE No. 39
"The Puerto Rican Rum Mutation"

[Kaiju] Science Taskforce
[CASE F]ILE No. 37
[Case of] the Lost Demon Mine"

Kaiju Scienc[e Taskforce]
CASE FILE No. 122
"Case of the Samoan Tikibeast"

THE GIANT KILLERS. During the 1950s the Kaiju Science Taskforce discovered and exterminated many of the "naturally" occurring kaiju that plagued earth.

CHRIST, MY ONLY BUSINESS WITH THE TASKFORCE WAS TO SMILE, ACT FRIENDLY, AND THEN...

...CUT ITS BALLS OFF WHEN NO ONE WAS LOOKING.

BUT, GODDAMN, YOU TRY SINKING AN ORGANIZATION WHEN YOU'RE DODGING ANTS THE SIZE OF BUSES THAT PUKE RADIOACTIVE SICK!

KEEGAN: So your entire role in all this was simply as part of a pissing contest between Dulles and the President? *Are you fucking kidding me?!*

HAMPTON: Hey, if it quacks like a duck, right? Except, if ya spend enough time around spies, you eventually learn nothing is simply what it seems. Hell, I dunno...maybe it really was just a pissing contest in the beginning, but Allen wasn't fucking around. He was ready to have Tsubaraya shoved into a pine box if necessary.

KEEGAN: But why? What is so damn special about the KST? To hear you tell it, Tsubaraya and his bunch were just killing rogue monsters to study them. *Wait...* That's it, isn't it?! *The monsters!* This whole damn thing is about kaiju...or rather, *kaiju secrets!* Isn't it?! *Isn't it?!*

HAMPTON: I didn't know myself until 1959, but yeah. Allen, or rather the men Allen answered to, didn't want Ike (or anybody else) fitting the pieces together. Ever wonder why UFO sightings in America were about zero before July 16, 1945? One word, my friend: Trinity. That was the day we hatched the big guy, Fat Man. When we unlocked the secrets of the beast, our skies were suddenly full of weird lights and saucers. James Forrestal, he knew why, and he was gonna talk. Instead, he took a fatal trip out a hospital window.

HAMPTON: Excuse me? Who?

HAMPTON: Truman's guy, James Forrestal—first ever Secretary of Defense. He wanted to go public about the men from Mars in '49. Then somebody tossed his ass out a window at the Naval Medical Center in Bethesda. Dropped him sixteen floors, smack into rock hard concrete.

KEEGAN: Somebody as in your people?

HAMPTON: Doubtful. That was back when Admiral Hillen-koetter was still helming the CIA, back when the Company still saw itself as an over-glorified version of Naval Intelligence. Wasn't until Dulles took the reins that things turned dirty. Plus, Washington didn't become a shooting gallery until Nixon.

KEEGAN: Quick to defend the home team, aren't you?

HAMPTON: There's no love lost between me and the Company, if that's what you're thinking.

KEEGAN: What I'm thinking is that I still don't trust you. And like, maybe, I'm being had. You just have all the answers, don't you? That is, except when we start getting close to your own culpability. Then it's anyone's guess, isn't it? Know what's wrong with this picture, Hampton? You. Your hands are too clean for someone whose been down in the muck with the dogs and pigs.

HAMPTON: "...and they looked from pig to man, and man to pig, and from pig to man again; but already it was impossible to say which was which." Kid, all of us are down in the muck—even you. Only difference is I ain't pretending to be spotless. How am I blowin' smoke up your ass? Just what is it you think I'm dodging?

KEEGAN: The Kaiju Science Taskforce. Your role as an agency stooge. You must've...

HAMPTON: What it is you think I did, *boy?*

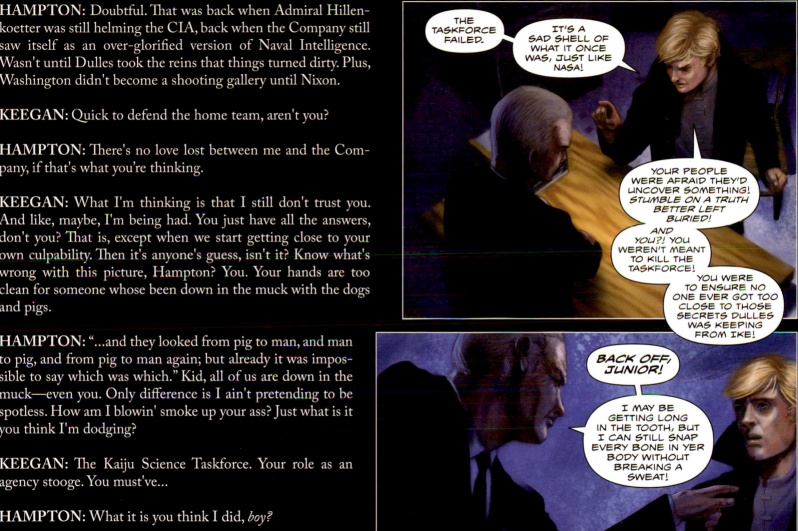

KEEGAN: Listen, man, I'm tired of all your phoney cloak and dagger newspeak. No more games, Hampton... *I want facts!* I *need* to know what *you* know.

HAMPTON: And what is it you think I know? The formula to Coke? Where to find Hoffa? What?

KEEGAN: You can start by coming clean about the Kaiju Science Taskforce. What was your mission? What were you really sent to do? I want the god's honest truth.

HAMPTON: Ain't a damn thing that's come out of my mouth yet that's been false, boy. If you ain't hearing the answers you want, maybe its because you're not asking the right questions.

KEEGAN: Alright. What was going on behind the scenes? The CIA clearly felt it vital to have a mole inside the KST, so when you'd report back to your people, what did you tell them? What did they say to you? If I were a fly on the wall, what would I have heard?

HAMPTON: Honestly? How much I wanted out of the goddamn job.

...CONSIDER STRANGE?

KAIJU SCIENCE TASKFORCE, CASE FILE No. 13: "The Case of the Howgill Leapist." In the Scottish Highlands a cult of neo-druids were discovered sacrificing tax collectors to an atomic mutant.

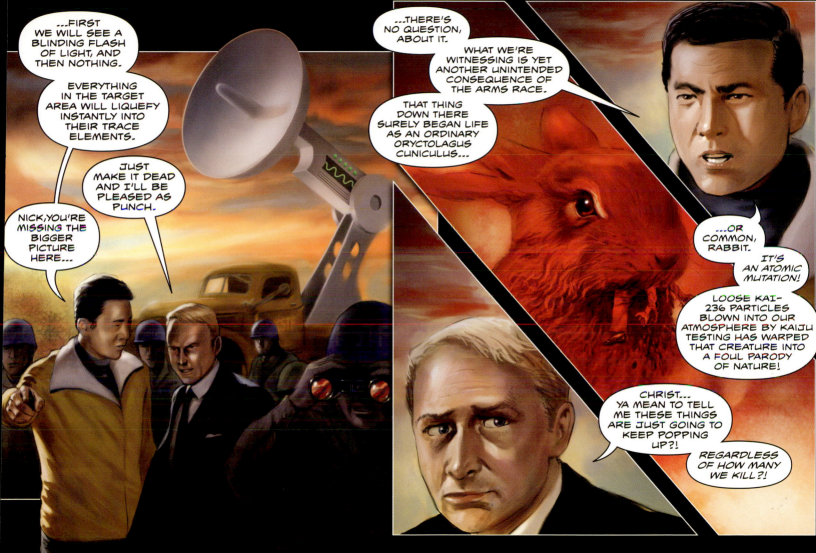

Zzzzz.

SAW A LOT OF WEIRD STUFF WHEN I WAS WITH THE TASKFORCE.

KILLED A LOT OF IT, TOO.

BUT IT WASN'T UNTIL THE SUMMER OF '56 THAT I GOT SOMETHING OF A NOTION...

HAMPTON: ...of what The Company meant when they asked me to keep an eye out for anything strange. Up in Barrow, Alaska, a USGS survey team had found something...*a kaiju*... buried in the ice.

SURVEY A-1355.2
> SITE #047

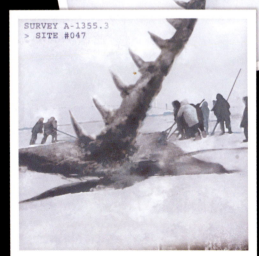

SURVEY A-1355.3
> SITE #047

KEEGAN: Frozen?

HAMPTON: Yeah. Was just like them wooly mammoths that were dug up in Berezovka... this kaiju, it was a left over from the last ice age.

KEEGAN: And this is what your pals at the CIA were so jittery about?

HAMPTON: Maybe. Or, it could've been what was found along side the monster. According to the survey team's report there was something else in the ice. Something big, something metal...a thing that eventually came to be known simply as *the artifact.*

KEEGAN: Was that a code name? Or, was it an artifact in the sense that it was the kind of thing I could see at a natural history museum?

HAMPTON: Dunno. I never saw the thing. By the time the Science Taskforce arrived on site, it and the monster were...

KEEGAN: The whole town?

HAMPTON: Everyone. A population of nine hundred plus people...rig jockeys, geologists, Eskimos...all gone like the earth had just opened up and swallowed 'em. Lights were on in homes, food on the table gone cold. Cars were in the streets, keys in the ignition. One of the creepiest damn things I ever did see.

KEEGAN: But how? The logistics alone would of something like...

HAMPTON: Ya know what the problem with the truth is? It's not obliged to stick to what's accepted as possible or even real. Truth is stranger than fiction. Ya know why? Fiction...fiction needs to make sense.

KEEGAN: Are we approaching another one of those moments where you'll tell me some far out cosmic revelation about how aliens are living like Indians in an Arizona nudist park and then you try to convince me I'm a chump for not taking your word for it?

HAMPTON: Actually it's Utah that they like. It's the volcanic soil there. Something about it reminds them of old Mars, back in the days before it turned into a big red dustbowl.

KEEGAN: I... I... I'm at a loss, Hampton. Every time I think I've finally tuned into your signal, you turn up the crazy. *Do you hear this stuff?!* Is this all part of some routine you scripted out before coming here? Or, am I just witnessing a bizarre form of improv? Because everything I know about...

HAMPTON: *Everything you know is wrong!* You're looking for secrets, but you're digging in all the wrong places. Take a step back! Look around you! This ain't our country anymore! There hasn't been an honest election here since 1968! And if you kids don't get your act together we're going to have another damn war on our hands!

KEEGAN: You know what, Hampton? I was going to say, "We're done here." But no, not this time. This time we're doing things my way.

HAMPTON: Oh, are we now?

KEEGAN: Goddamn right, we are.

HAMPTON: Alright, cowboy. You get on that horse. Let's see where it takes you.

KEEGAN: What'll happen is you're going to cut to the chase. Instead of you trying to convince me, I want to hear from you exactly what it was that opened *your* eyes. I want to know what transformed a supposedly straight arrow government man like yourself into a true believer.

HAMPTON: A true believer, huh?

C'MON, OLD MAN!

WHATEVER YOU SAW, IF IT WAS ENOUGH TO CONVINCE YOU...

...SHOULD BE ENOUGH TO CONVINCE A LOWLY CIVVIE LIKE ME!

KENNEDY.

SEEING A PRESIDENT'S BRAINS SPRAYED ALL OVER HIS FIRST LADY...

...AND KNOWING WHO PULLED THE TRIGGER AND WHY.

NVASION USA!

GREAT SCOTT! COMMIE TANKS HAVE INVADED AMERICA! HOW CAN THEY EVER BE STOPPED!? EASY! YOU SEND IN...

...THE MIGHTY *FAT MAN!* YES, AMERICA'S GREATEST KAIJU HERO, FAT MAN! IN YOUR OWN HOME!!

USE *FAT MAN'S* AMAZING SPRING-LOADED ROCKET FIST...

...TO SMASH THE DIABOLICAL RED ARMY!

KEEN!

Batteries Not Included.

OR SCORCH 'EM WITH *FAT MAN'S* FIERCE FIRE BREATH! PULL THE HANDLE AND SEE THE GLOW OF HIS KAIJU POWER!

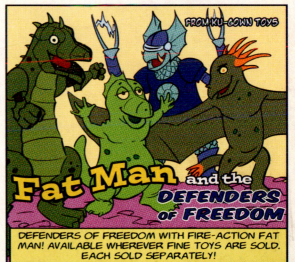

FROM KU-COWN TOYS

Fat Man and the DEFENDERS of FREEDOM

"Mummy, what happens to us if the monsters come?"

She looks to you for a real answer. She knows what she must do when the sirens sound at school. But what happens if they sound when she's at home? Will YOU be ready, like her teacher is? Are you ready to protect her from harm. Ready to help her if she is hurt?

A kaiju attack is something like the scariest parts of the Old Testament. Expect fires, floods, and the invisible plague of radiation—all at once! Everyone needs to be prepared!

U. S. Civil Defense, working with doctors and kaiju scientists, has developed a list of "must have" disaster aid supplies. These few simple items may already be in your home or, if not, you can get them at any drug counter. For the sake of your children, your neighbors, and yourself, these supplies should be in your home—and you should know how to use them.

We are all in this together. Are you doing your part?

BE SURE TO HAVE THESE OFFICIAL DISASTER ITEMS

☐ Gas Masks

☐ Rubber Gloves

☐ Sterile Gauze Pads

☐ Large Emergency Dressing

☐ 100 Water-Purification Tablets

☐ Sodium Chloride Tablets

☐ Antiseptic (Benzalkonium Chloride)

☐ Valium Pills and/or Flask Of Hard Liquor

☐ Potassium Iodine Tablets

☐ Cyanide Pills

☐ Body Bags

PROJECT ANVIL

STUDY PREPARED BY THE ATOMIC ENERGY COMMISSION

1948-1952

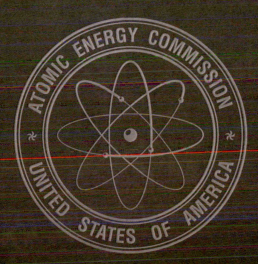

Printed for the use of the White House.

LOS ALAMOS
SANTA FE. NEW MEXICO
P.O. BOX 1663

10/22/1952

President of the U.S.A.
The White House
Washington, D.C.

Mister President,

As per your request, I have compiled an overview of the A.E.C.'s Project Anvil findings. I believe you will find it enlightening. It should answer many of your questions about these amazing creatures. My colleagues and I have worded this document in layman's terms to the best of our ability. If you have any questions or require more detailed information, I am available for direct counsel at any time.

I look forward to our next meeting.

Best regards,

Robert Oppenheimer

-J. Robert Oppenheimer, PhD.
Chief Science Advisor
Atomic Energy Commission

PROJECT ANVIL: An Overview

Since 1948 the Atomic Energy Commission has conducted a long-term study of kaiju with the stated goal of building a comprehensive understanding of kaiju biology, psychology, and all related physics. *Codenamed: Project Anvil*, a team of the nation's best minds have been tasked with the research. In 1950 Anvil's scope was extended to include applied sciences, which is now being overseen by John von Neumann (M.I.T.) and Akira Tsubaraya (Hiroshima University). Later in 1952, Anvil officially came under the wing of the newly established Kaiju Science Taskforce. Herein is an overview of Project Anvil's findings.

For ease of reading, this document is separated into seven distinct categories:

[1] Lexicon
[2] Atomo-Genesis
[3] KAI-235
[4] Kaiju Basics
[5] Taxonomy
[6] Psychology
[7] Command & Control

Contributors:
J. Robert Oppenheimer, Albert Einstein, Werner Karl Heisenberg, Akira Tsubaraya, John von Neumann, John H. Manley, Enrico Fermi, Harold Carpenter Hodge, Alasdair Stuart, Mohammed Khan, J.C. Baron.

[1] LEXICON: Scientific Terminology

Kaijuology is a very young and wholly unique science. Because of this, new terminology has entered the scientific lexicon to better describe these creatures. Collected here is a list of the most current kaiju-specific words and phrases.

Atomic Heart: A semi-organic organ that is unique to kaiju. This organ fuels the kaiju's cardiovascular system byway of bio-atomic fission.

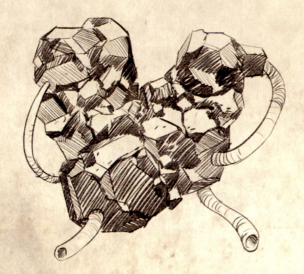

Atomo-Genesis: The unique form of atomic fission-based parthenogenesis from which kaiju are born.

Bioform: Due to their artificial birthing and hybrid cell structure, kaiju are considered bioforms rather than true living, breathing lifeforms. NOTE: While this designation is a scientific one, we do hope this distinction will help calm the more religious members of congress.

Dirty: Refers to a KAI-235 crystal that is structurally impure, or "dirty" with cracks, flaws, and mineral deposits. Dirty crystals are called as such for their dull, milky appearance.

Dirty Hatching: Any hatching which uses an impure KAI-235 crystal to trigger atomogenesis. These hatchings, although cheaper and easier, are more likely to fail and always spawn malformed beasts.

Junk Kaiju: Vernacular for a kaiju spawned from a dirty hatching. Also called "bargain kaiju."

PsyCAp: Short for Psychotronic Control Apparatus. Most NATO and Russian kaiju are controlled via PsyCAp devices which broadcast and receive tuned psionic waves.

Psychotronic: Psychic technology.

Pure: Refers to a structurally intact KAI-235 crystal, meaning that the crystal lattice is perfectly formed and is free of cracks, flaws, or mineral deposits. A pure crystal is easily identified by its perfect gemlike shape and luster.

Rejdák: A unit of measurement for psychic waves. The Rejdák scale is named after Soviet physicist Zdeněk Rejdák, founder of psychotronic research.

Rogue Kaiju: Any beast that is not under the control of a nation, military, or recognized military power. Most rogue kaiju are assumed to be free roaming and under no form of control, although the Mohdrah Incident suggests some rogue kaiju are at least guided by some form of external manipulation.

SpoGeM: Short for SPOntaneously-GEnerated Monster. It is unknown how or why kaiju are beginning to spontaneously occur in nature, but it is a phenomena that is happening with increased frequency. Doctor Tsubaraya theorizes the cause may be linked to increased levels of loose KAI-235 radiation in Earth's atmosphere, which has increased exponentially in recent years since the United States and Russia began growing their kaiju arsenals.

MONSTER 10

In this day and age nearly everyone knows where kaiju come from—they are the result of splitting of atoms within a KAI-235 isotope matrix. However, the actual processes behind atomo-genesis remain shrouded behind the highest levels of national security. Thanks to a well orchestrated campaign of misinformation by the Department of Defense, most of the world believes these creatures spring forth from irradiated crystals the same way a chick does from an egg. In reality, the process is far more miraculous, and unlike anything witnessed in nature. A kaiju "hatching" manifests in rapid conversion of energy to self-arranging matter.

Atomo-genesis happens in four phases:

Phase I: Catalyst
A free neutron is fired into the nucleus of a KAI-235 atom causing its crystal lattice to split. This releases a cascade of more free neutrons.

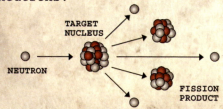

NEUTRON

TARGET NUCLEUS

FISSION PRODUCT

Phase II: Chain-Reaction
The neutron cascade splits more of the crystal lattice, creating a domino-effect. In less than a fraction of a second this chain reaction forces the entire KAI crystal to collapse, releasing a burst of powerful energy.

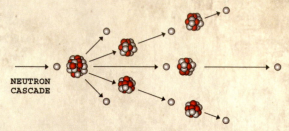

NEUTRON CASCADE

Phase III: Transmutation
The polarity of the neutron flow reverses, triggering transmutation. The released energy is rapidly converted into semi-organic matter and then self-arranges into a fully-developed bioform.

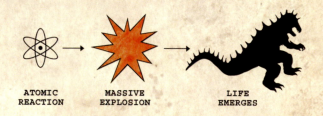

ATOMIC REACTION

MASSIVE EXPLOSION

LIFE EMERGES

Phase IV: Synchronization
The brain of the newly-formed kaiju is linked and synced with its psychotronic

command apparatus (PsyCAp) and then brought under control.

As first discovered at Trinity, a critical mass of the isotope is required for Phase I to occur—specifically a pure KAI-235 crystal weighing no less than 15 kilograms (33 pounds). Hatching can also be achieved with an impure crystal of greater mass, but always results in an unstable, defect-ridden beast (see section: Junk Kaiju).

Once Phase II is achieved energy is released in the form of a highly destructive explosion, plus intense radiation. The D.O.D. has gone to great lengths to downplay the dangers of kaiju hatching to both the public and Congress. This is necessary and understandable. But in light of recent risks taken at the Alamogordo test site, it is the determination of the A.E.C. that neither the Pentagon nor the Administration truly appreciate the dangers of our kaiju

weapons program. For instance, the hatching of Fat Man released a blast equivalent to 35,440 tons of TNT (35 kilotons). As unbelievable as that reads, this is not in error. Einstein has calculated that the force released in a hatching is directly proportional to the amount of energy a kaiju's atomic heart generates.

It is critical to note that although our kaiju program has eff...

Mister President-

Regarding the high-yield explosions caused during kaiju hatchings. It has come to my attention that Ed Teller has been proposing America develop a bomb based on these "atomic" explosions. I must contend with my colleagues, Einstein and Heisenberg, that this path of research must not be pursued, a sentiment that has been echoed by Sec. of Defense Forrestal. A global kaiju war would lay waste to every city on the planet, but a war of Teller's "atom bombs" would escalate to such a level of apocalyptic destruction that there would be no one left to recover from it.

Please understand, Mister President, we have entered a very exciting yet precarious new age of scientific development. We have stolen from the gods the power of creation and destuction. At no time should we take this for granted.

-Oppenheimer

[3] KAI-235

Prior to the modern era, the KAI-235 isotope was considered little more than a geologic oddity. In fact, throughout the 19th Century the few crystals that had been unearthed either found their way into museums or the collections of the very rich. KAI crystals were also highly sought after by spiritualists, who referred to the isotopes as "specter stones" due to their haunting green glow. It was believed these crystals contained the captured souls of D'Jinn (evil spirits), and that possessing one would increase a seer's power. Then in 1936 an unknown German scientist hit upon the fantastic notion that the glow inside a KAI crystal was a unique energy state that could be transmuted into life. Three years later Hitler placed Dr. Werner Heisenberg at the helm of Project Fenris, which aimed to unlock the secrets of KAI-235 for use as a weapon. **(see Appendix 5.2c "CIA: Project Paperclip")**

And as they say, the rest is history.

Contrary to popular belief, KAI crystal deposits are not rare. Trace amounts of the stone can be found in most sediment around the world, but it is usually fused with local minerals to the point of being unrecognizable. Even pure stones found in nature tend to be no larger than a marble and do not glow. What is hard to come by is fissionable KAI isotopes. A pure KAI crystal must weigh a minimum of 15 kilograms to be converted into a functioning bioform.

Since the beginning of the Arms Race, the Pentagon has taken some comfort in the knowledge that pure crystals are difficult to obtain in most parts of the world. Nations such as India, Iran, Iraq, and China have plentiful KAI deposits, but fortunately lack the sophisticated mining techniques to recover them. Unfortunately, the same cannot be said for the Soviet Union, where vast crystal fields are said to be sitting atop the Siberian tundra.

[4] KAIJU BASICS

Aside from a handful of anatomical common-
alities, all kaiju are unique creatures. No
unifying species or genotype has ever been
identified. For a bioform to be classified
as a "true" kaiju it must meet the follow-
ing requirements:

1. Atomo-Genesis

All kaiju are spawned by way of atomo-
genesis, which as stated before, requires
splitting the atoms of a KAI-235 crystal
that is 15 kilograms or more. Bioforms have
been created from smaller mass KAI crystals, but are not kaiju in that they lack
an atomic heart **(see Appendix, 32.11a
"Codename: Little Boy")**.

"Little Boy"

2. Size Limit

Kaiju physiology requires a minimum
weight-to-mass to maintain its internal
atomic fission. Ten metric tons appears to
be the critical cut-off. Because of this,
most kaiju tend to stand anywhere between
20 and 80 meters tall.

Big Ben   Fat Man

3. Mule

All kaiju are genetic mules and therefore
lack the means to reproduce. According to
the NATO intelligence briefs Soviet scientists have made numerous attempts to engi-
neer a fertile kaiju. To date, there is no
evidence to suggest these experiments have
been anything short of disastrous **(see
Appendix, 22.5g "The Siberian Snow Monkey
Incident")**.

4. Genetically Random

Unlike the creatures of the natural world,
kaiju cannot be categorized in terms of

kingdom, phylum, class, etc. Aside from rare instances of twin hatching **(see Appendix, 02.65w "Atomo-Genesis Anomalies")**, no two kaiju are genetically similar enough to be classed into specific breeds as we do with true animals. Each beast is a unique bioform unto itself. For this reason kaiju taxonomy is based on apparent dominant traits and not genetic similarities.

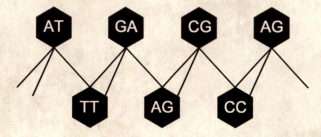

5. Radioactive

The kaiju cardiovascular system is fueled by a form of bio-atomic fission. While this process is not fully understood, we do know it is the key to their physiology. Without the vast amounts of energy supplied by an atomic heart, creatures of such size and power simply could not function. Conversely, an unfortunate side-effect of this is radioactivity. All beasts emit varying amounts of deadly radiation. This output rises proportionally to a beast's physical activity.

6. Meltdown Risk

Although highly efficient, bio-atomic fission is not without its problems. In theory, larger kaiju run the risk of a thermal meltdown when too much strain is placed on its atomic heart. While this has never been tested, Einstein predicts a bio-fission meltdown would result in a blast roughly equivalent to a beast's kilotonnage.

Saurian
Frequency: 25%
Kaiju whose dominant traits resemble clas-
sic dinosaurs. Saurians are the most
common of all kaiju. It is estimated one in
every four beasts walking the Earth today
is of this type. More curious is that
roughly 75% of all non-saurian kaiju show
at least some saurian traits, such as
scales or a ridged vertebrae. This leads
credence to Dr. Vannevar Bush's theory that
kaiju are not naturally occurring life, but
engineered and that the saurian-type serves
as a sort of base model from which all
kaiju are built upon.

Insectoid
Frequency: 18%
This is the second most common kaiju type.
Despite what the name implies, this classification refers to kaiju with bug-like
traits. This includes not only insects, but
also arachnids, centipedes and millipedes.

Mammaloid
Frequency: 16%
Mammaloid are interesting in that they
rarely, if ever, resemble any known mammal.
These beasts always form as a jumble of
mammalian traits, the most common of these
being: fur, horns, webbed wings, cropped
ears, and snouts. Also unlike most kaiju,
which tend toward a bipedal configuration,
~55% of all mammaloids spawn as quadrupeds.

Reptillicus
Frequency: 12%
Often mistaken for saurians, reptillicus
beasts are distinctly different in that
they are akin to modern day reptiles. This
is especially pronounced in bone structure
and a tendency to almost always be quadrupeds. Other defining traits include: forked
tongues, three digit claws, lack of eye-
lids, and whip-like tails. It should be
noted it is very rare for kaiju not to have
limbs. While snake-like features are not
uncommon with reptillicus beasts, an actual
limbless snake bioform has never occurred.

Cephalopod
Frequency: 9%

Usually squid, cuttlefish, and octopus type creatures, but extends to include any kaiju with a tentacle based body structure. Curiously, despite their aquatic appearance, cephalopod types rarely use their tentacles for swimming. In fact, most either levitate or are land-based creatures that slither or crawl. More often than not, a cephalopod's tendrils develop as weapons rather than a means of locomotion.

Simian
Frequency: 8%

Simians are clearly ape-like. Most tend to favor mammaloid or saurian secondary traits which give them a hulking "monster-man" appearance. In a few cases, though, hatchings have resulted in kaiju that almost resemble a modern day gorilla or silverback ape. Simians tend to be smaller beasts and rarely stand more than 30 feet. They also rarely develop exotic abilities such as breath weapons, flight, or energy projection.

Draconis
Frequency: 5%

Also often mistaken for saurians, draconis kaiju resemble mythological dragons and sea monsters. In fact, the likeness is so striking it does raise the question: were monsters of legend actually what we call rogue kaiju today? One argument against this is a lack of fossil evidence, which surely would have been uncovered by now. This logical assertion does overlook one key point—we have no data regarding the average lifespan of a kaiju. Kaiju are also known to sleep/hibernate for years at a time if left inactive. The dragons of legend may very well be some of the rogue beasts we are dealing with today. Clearly, more research is needed.

President Eisenhower,

I urge you to read my report on the simian-type kaiju codenamed Gargantuan. Your military has locked the creature in the Yucca Mountain Hibernation Unit for safety reasons. They claim he is too intelligent and too difficult to control. This may be true, but I believe study of this kaiju is required. My initial research on test samples has suggested Gargantuan may share a common ancestry with mankind. To look at him, you can see he does indeed have an almost proto-human or Neanderthal appearance.

Sadly, I have been barred from further study of Gargantuan by Brigadier General Nichols. He insists that some things "are better left unknown" and that a link between kaiju and humans may be "too much for the god-fearing public to handle."

—Akria Tsubaraya

Crustacean
Frequency: 5%

Kaiju that resemble shellfish. While kaiju with lobster and crab features are quite common, for a beast to be considered a true crustacean-type requires a full exoskeleton. From a military standpoint these beasts are a mixed blessing. Crustaceans tend to spawn from high kilotonnage hatchings, therefore are usually immensely powerful. Unfortunately, these kaiju are also as stupid as they are clumsy. This makes crustacean-types hard to control. This is not due to the creature resisting its orders, but rather difficulty understanding them.

Grabboid
Frequency: 2%

Describes all worm, snail, slug, and mollusk type kaiju. Aside from occasionally developing whip-like antenna, these creatures do not have limbs of any kind. Predictably this makes them lacking in terms of physicality. Conversely, grabboids nearly always spawn having a projectile, spray, or beam weapon. Mandibles are also common.

Amorphous
Frequency: Occurs in 50% of dirty hatchings

Also known as a blob-type, these beasts are exactly as the name implies—a kaiju that lacks a coherent shape. Some are moving acid puddles, others are ambulatory slime molds. The most common, though, are blob-like mounds with randomly placed limbs and sense organs. In actuality the amorphous classification is not a true kaiju type, but the result of a very flawed dirty hatching. All kaiju types listed here can be considered amorphous if it is spawned with excessive deformities.

Ichthyian
Frequency: Unknown

Ichthian, or fish-type kaiju, so far only exist in theory. With the sheer number of known kaiju with fish-like secondary features, it is suspected a beast with dominant fish traits must be at least possible. Unfortunately, until an ichthian-type is actually hatched this is pure speculation.

[5] PSYCHOLOGY

Kaiju brains vary greatly, thus there is no standard model for the mental processes of these creatures. Some beasts, such as Fat Man, are clearly self-aware and even demonstrate what some might call a personality. In fact, Admiral Radford has proposed that it is not Fat Man's raw power that makes him such a formidable weapon, but rather his ability to think creatively on the battlefield. While some kaiju operate on a purely instinctual level, Fat Man has exibited a fighting style akin to Greco-Roman wrestling.

KAIJU
BRAIN

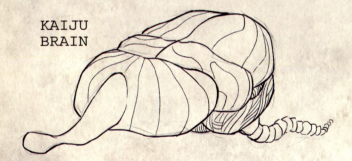

Conversely, the USAF's 22 kiloton flier, Razor Beak, has a distinctly primal based consciousness. Or as one Air Force colonel once put it, "Controlling the crazy son of a bitch is like trying to walk a rabid dog on a leash." This was certainly demonstrated during the infamous Mohdrah Inci

dent (see Appendix, 71.8f "Battle of Manhattan"). During the 23 minute aerial battle with Mohdrah, Razor Beak effectively caused more damage to Manhattan Island than the enemy.

Fat Man has dem

Sir,

    In the spring of 1952 the Atomic Energy Commission was asked to supply the newly formed Central Intelligence Agency with a lesser kaiju for "research purposes." We acquired the five kiloton beast, Glomeris, on lend from the Army. Since that time my collogues and I have heard rumblings about the C.I.A. using the beast for psychotropic drug experiments with the intent of creating a new means of kaiju control. These methods strike me as highly questionable, but it is not my place to judge. The least I ask is for the C.I.A. to share their findings and to return Glomeris. On the second point, the Army has been very insistent about this—the generals want their monster back.

    At first, the C.I.A. refused to do so. After several more phone calls the agency claimed to have never received Glomeris at all. In an attempt to track the monster down I sent a request to the General Accounting Office. The best they could tell me was that "...the Army's giant Pill Bug was somewhere in Cambodia." Please, General Miller is becoming increasing irate. If the Administration could assist in resolving the issue as soon as possible, it would help greatly.

                — John von Neumann

[6] COMMAND & CONTROL

Even more coveted than the secrets of Atomo-Genesis are the means of kaiju control. A common misconception is that kaiju are operated in a manner similar to a child's remote-control toy. In the field of cybernetics, this kind of remote piloting is what is called *Direct Feedback Control* (DFC). For weaponized kaiju, a direct feedback system has become something of a Holy Grail. Every nation wants it, but none have yet successfully created a means to do so.

In reality, kaiju are not piloted. They are operated by way of *Variable Feedack Control* (VFC) systems. Put simply, "variable" is a less terrifying way of saying these monsters have minds of their own. Orders are carried out only insofar as a monster can understand them. Or worse, insofar as they are willing to cooperate. More "spirited" kaiju have and will ignore commands entirely. During tests at the Nevada Proving Groud, Fat Man showed a distinct unwillingness to attack targets he found uninteresting. If it wasn't big, flashy, or moving, Fat Man did not want to be bothered with it. More troubling were tests with the primal-minded Razor Beak. Twice during live-fire exercises, this flying kaiju frenzied and became unable to distinguish between friendly and hostile targets.

The key to all methods of kaiju control is a monster's manomaya stone. This is a fist-sized red crystal that is produced simultaniously with the beast during the hatching. The manomaya shares a telepathic resonance with its monster, and is required for a control device to work.

Described here are all currently known methods for kaiju control.

Psychotronic Control Apparatus

At first glance a PsyCAp device looks much like one of our UNIVAC computers. These enormous machines are able to transmit orders to a kaiju by way of psychotronic waves. Commands are given in a mathematical language which is then interpreted by the kaiju. The complexity of these orders are based entirely on the creatures own intelligence. The dumber the monster, the greater the risk of a misunderstanding.

Although, a kaiju that is "too smart" will often strain the parameters of a given order, or even outright ignore it. Currently PsyCAp technology requires the device be within 100 miles of its kaiju to work effectively.

to the monster's limbs and body by remote.

The Shock Harness has had a mixed operational record. It functions best with docile kaiju with minimal intelligence. The more self-aware a kaiju is, the less likely it will cooperate. Also, when used with more primal minded kaiju, the painful zaps from a shock harness have been known to cause the monster to frenzy.

Shock Harness

Also known as the "electric marionette," the Shock Harness was the first serious attempt at a direct feedback control device. A series of high-voltage electrodes are riveted to the kaiju's dermis, which is then wired to a collar that siphons electricity from the creature's heart. Control is achieved by sending electric shocks directly

KAIJU TEST DUMMY

Psychotronic Helmet

While American hatching technology has clearly outpaced the Soviet Union, we cannot even begin to compete with Russian psychotronics. Most Russian monsters still require a PsyCAp device, but they are not given commands in a mathematical programming language. Instead, orders are transmitted "sympathetically" by a trained telepath wearing a psycho-helmet. This allows for a greater level of control over a beast. This method also seems to foster greater levels of cooperation from the more intelligent monsters.

Astro-Kong wearing the neural remote

Neural Remote

Still in the experimental stage, Dr. Von Neumann's neural remote project could eventually produce an effective means of direct feedback control. The device works on the principle of wiring control relays into a monster's brain, which accepts commands from remote. So far, this method has only been tested on the third Yucca Flats hatching, Codename: Astro-Kong. Results have shown promise, with one major caveat—the neural remote appears to have driven Astro-Kong completely batty (for lack of a better word).

TEAM KAIJU!
Elite Kickstarter Action Response Force

Jeremy Rathbone of the Lost World
Adam Thibault the Giant Claw
King Kitka: The Towering Terror
The Deadly Might of Ihimu Ukpo
The Colossal Comfort Love & Adam Withers
The Mighty Joe Kontor
Mike J Fratus Jr. from 20,000 Fathoms
Grady W. Smithey III, the Monolith Monster
James Dean Merrill from Green Hell
Melissa Aho the 50 Foot Woman
Karl Wasmuth of Planet X
David Goldstein the Colossal Beast
Chrustopher Michael Rosa the Behemoth
Mary Kathryn Hammond the Sea Monster
Glenn Like the Giant Gila Monster
The Kaiju Killer R. Zemlicka
Mac McClintock of the Mysterious Island
Mike Sloup the Space Monster
Diarra Kenyon Harris the Three-Headed Monster
Alan Irwin the Astro-Monster
Wrath of the Giant Daryl Mukai
Kevin Derendorf the Magic Serpent
Evette Langford the Gargantua
Matthew Jennings, Monster from the Deep
Derek Coward from Outer Space
Cliff the Mighty
William Ellis the Giant Space Amoeba
The Unstoppable Scott "Bolverkloki" Taylor
Jeremy Wiggins the Atomic Death Frog

Stephanie Wagner the Lepus
Matt Cline the Giant Spider
Terror of Charles J. O'Boyle III
Micheal Dodds: Super Monster
D.Cooper the Psychotic Death Gator
Marc A. Tanenbaum the Iron Titan
Jeff Christner the Winged Serpent
Karl Markovich the Monster Shark
Hunter Zimmerman: Guardian of the Universe
Emad Hasan the Super Raptor
Richard Archer the Dreaded Kraken
William I. Johnson the Atomic Dinocroc
Ninja Force Shean, Semeicha & Sapphira Mohammed, Go!
Ryan Lake the Psycho Piranha
Eric Steven Johnson, Deep Sea Beast
Rick & Charlene Brandon the Brave
William Goodell Jr. is Monster Zero!
Colby Miller the Giant Mantis
Tim Vargulish Ferocious Giant Iron Invader
Rob Breadon the Death Worm
Tyrnn Eaveranth of the Morlocks
Ray Layton the Giant Killer Eye
Dale Stephen Schue the Moon Beast
Alex Thornton-Clark: Attack of Legion
Joe Beam the Flying Mutant Python
Keith Houin, Toxic Titanic Komodo
Riley McIlvaine the Radioactive Cobra
Michael J. Wistock of the Bigfoots
Mega Cat Stark
The Terror of Mecha Nick Keist
R. Scott Daniels the Radium Pterodactyl
Seth Roman Witucki the Eight Legged Freak
Monster Master John Harter - Waterfront Comics

Tim Baldwin: The Monster from Mars
Crocosaurus Troy Miller-Perry
Swamp Shark Chalmrah
Death Lord Alp Aziz Torun
Apostolis Dousias the Crawling Eye
Christopher Burdett of Loch Ness
Dotan Dvir the Killer Snow Monkey
Shawn McKinney of the Deep
MegaZone: Realm of Terror
Jasmine Wolf the Spawn of Fenris
Joseph M. McDermott the Mighty Mega Mammoth
Paul Spence the Beast Out of Time
Emma Chester: The Revenge of Iris
James Chamberlain the Giant Moussaka
Michael Canavan: Fist of Doom
The Flying Horror of Noe J. Medina
Steven Callen the Robo Raptor from Hell
Mzy McCants the Total Berzerker
Jay Bandoy the Nuclear Sand Shark
Martin Mueller of the Mysterious Island
Nadine Valkenberg the Giant Slayer
Techno Terror Tim Gessler
Jennifer Lundquist of Red Mars
Kyle Johnson of the Black Lagoon
Matthew E. Walker the Unbelievable!
Frank because he is called Frank
Jonathan Pelletier the Moon Wolf
Adam G. Hults the Aztec Mummy
Ernie Pelletier, Friendly Neighborhood Comics
Jarrad Speed the Man Made Monster
Rich "Sentaison" Shirley the Crater Lake Monster
Hassan Murray Frog Monster from Hell
Grizzly Adam: Killer Kodiak

Jo Bangphraxay: The Queen of Outerspace!
Kevin Frees the Dark Intruder
David Conner: Guardian of the Galaxy
Ryan Hillis the Deadly Spawn
Jemal Cole: Troll Hunter
Daniel Laloggia the Incredible
Johnathan Munroe the Immortal Monster
Ken Liu: Creature with the Atomic Brain
Jason Olexa the Giant Gila Monster
Alvin Yue of the Dark Side of the Moon
Damian Smith: Lord Shaper of Eldritch Horror
John Falcon Winged Monster from 17,000 BC
Cookie Palmiter: Terror from Beyond Space
Philip Skrzeczynski the Invisible Invader
Matt Frank the Beast of Yucca Flats
Justin W. Lee of Spider Island
Eric Jason Ratcliffe the Manster
Mike Arnoult: Giant Machine Samurai
Donny Davis of Phantom Lake
Gretch Dragon the Death Bringer
Anthony M. Olver of the Alligator People
Christian Rivero the Giant Shiny-Man
Brandon Waggle the Deadly Mantis
The Indestructible Justin W. Lee
Erik Norman Berglund of Boggy Creek
Aric Thompson the Sun Demon
Muhammad Ahmad (Imran) Khan: Soul Crusher
Dave Walters the Monarch of Monsters
Robot Monster John Ostrosky Jr
Bruce Wallace Huber the Strange Beast
Callum Dean Barnes Shogun Warrior
The Deadly James Edward Reed
Bryan Mauney Sentai Jetman

Cody Dolan the Triphibian Monster
Flt Lt Colin Bell Super Robot Giganto
Elena Finney Endlich Emperoress of the Universe
Adrienne George the Iron King
Andy Campbell Squid Crusher
King Kevin Lansford the Destructor
Carol Hyne the Destroyer
Mike N the Brain Eater
Ling-Ann the Invincible
Space Monster Kenny D
Ashley Hobley Fire Maiden of Mars
Justin S. Davis the Yeti
Chris Weiss the Colossal Man
Alan Loboschefski the Abominable Snowman
Terence Chua the X from Outer Space
Space Phantom Lee Finney of Krankor
Adam Foidart of the Demon
Sean McGowan Death Hydra
Hegetaga Shadowdale the Star Creature
Richard O'Bry Monster A Go-Go
Dane Gobbo Jenkins the Steel Golem
Scott Halander from the Haunted Sea
Ryan Mullan the Creeping Terror
Shanesaw the Immortal Monster
Albert Lei of the Mysterians
Rich Laux the Astro-Zombies

Science Support Corps.

Jonathan Sharp - WWK Theme Song
Lance Axt - Voice Talent Extraordinaire
Sharlynn V. - Japanese Translator

Media Support

Kaijucast
http://kaijucast.com

The kaijuphile
www.kaijuphile.com

Planet X Control Room
www.planetxcontrolroom.com

Giant Freakin Robot
www.giantfreakinrobot.com

Kickstarter Conversations
www.kickstarter-conversations.com

The Wombmater
www.geeqshuq.com

War Rocket Ajax
www.warrocketpodcast.com

The Outhousers
www.theouthousers.com

The Science Fiction Show
www.myscifishow.com/

Kray Z Comics
www.krayzcomix.solitairerose.com

Adventures in Sci-Fi Publishing
www.adventuresinscifipublishing.com

THE VICE PIT
www.youtube.com/user/avicevids

Den of Geek
www.denofgeek.com

Bleeding Cool
www.bleedingcool.com